NANCY DREW

Still Sleuthing!

By Jen Funk Weber

New York   London   Toronto   Sydney

An imprint of Simon & Schuster Children's Publishing Division
1230 Avenue of the Americas, New York, NY 10020
NANCY DREW © 2007 Warner Bros. Entertainment Inc.
NANCY DREW is a registered trademark of Simon & Schuster, Inc. (s07)
SIMON SCRIBBLES and associated colophon are trademarks
of Simon & Schuster, Inc.
Manufactured in the United States of America
First Edition
2 4 6 8 10 9 7 5 3 1
ISBN-13: 978-1-4169-3381-6
ISBN-10: 1-4169-3381-6

MOVIE LINES

Boxes connected by lines contain the same letter. Some letters are given, while others have to be guessed. When you fill in all the boxes, you'll be able to read a line from the movie.

Can you guess whose line it is?

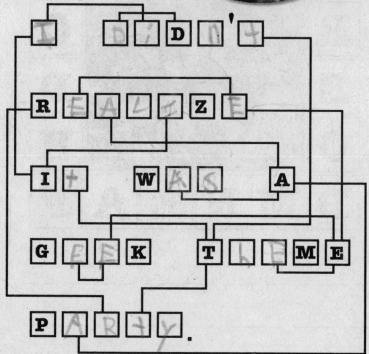

I DIDN'T

REALIZE

IT WAS A

GEEK THEME

PARTY.

Whose line is this? _____

3

While other students built coat hooks and bookends in wood shop, what did Nancy build?

To find out, start with a letter in one of the corners (no, we're not telling you which one), then read every third letter, clockwise around the square, until all letters are used.

C	A	R	A	L	E	E
T						T
R						O
E						D
O						H
D	M	N	E	A	F	F

Answer:

__ __ __ __ __ __ __

__ __ __ __ __ __ __

__ __ __ __

"Gumshoe" is another word for "detective."

Place the shoe words below into the grid so they crisscross like a crossword. We've done one to get you started.

4	**5**	**6**	**7**	**8**
BOOT	SLIDE	BALLET	HIGH TOP	ATHLETIC
CLOG	SLING	OXFORD	~~LOAFERS~~	MARY JANE
FLAT	THONG	SADDLE	SANDALS	MOCCASIN
MULE	WEDGE	SKATES	SLIPPER	PLATFORM
PUMP		T-STRAP		

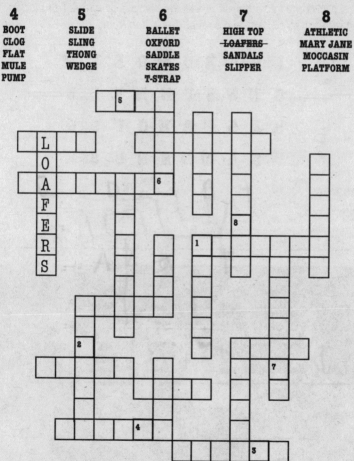

What shoes do spies wear? Write the letters in the numbered boxes on the spaces with the same numbers to find out.

__1__ __2__ __3__ __4__ __5__ __6__ __7__ __8__

(5)

It was there a minute ago, but now it's gone! Someone stole it!

To find out what was stolen, cross off every letter that appears three times (and only three times). Read the remaining letters from left to right and top to bottom to discover the stolen item.

```
I P A E U M G E K M
C N W S I H N W U E
K E G F A K O I L G
W S A M D E N U S R
```

Answer:

_____-_____ _____

An early clue to the Dehlia Draycott mystery was a letter she wrote to Z. Make your own letters memorable with stylin' stationery.

Materials

- 6 x 8 inch stationery with envelopes
- 1 spool $5/16$ inch wide ribbon (soft, flexible ribbon works best)
- Pencil
- Scissors
- Ruler
- Hole punch

1. Use ruler to draw a light line across one sheet of paper, ½ inch from top.

2. Mark a small x on the line ½ inch, 1½ inches, and 2½ inches from each side (6 marks in all).

3. Punch out each x with hole punch. (Punch 4 or 5 sheets at a time using ruled sheet as guide.)

4. Cut ribbon to 20 inches. Weave one end through three holes, starting from the back side at one edge, and working toward the middle. Weave other end of ribbon through remaining holes, starting from the back side and working from edge to middle. Ribbon ends should meet in the middle on the front. Adjust so ribbon ends are even lengths.

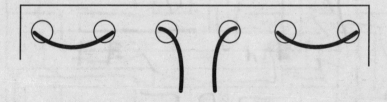

5. Tie ribbon ends into small bow. (It helps to put a heavy book or weight on the paper as you tie.) Cut away excess ribbon.

A SECRET PASSAGE

Leshing disappeared through a secret passage.

Can you help Nancy find him?

FOOTSTEPS

Nancy's hot on the heels of the mysterious "27" bandit. Follow in her footsteps to track him down.

The clues add up every step of the way, to a total of twenty-seven. Can you find the bandit's trail?

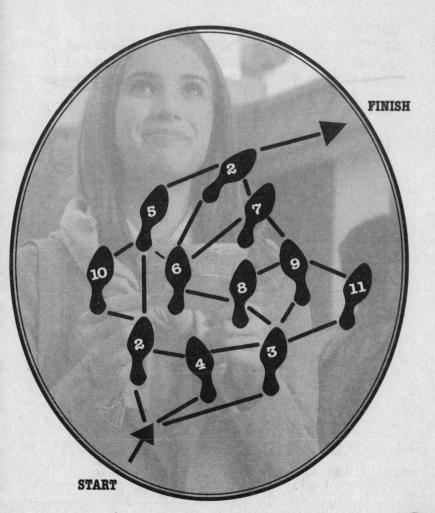

FINISH

START

**Nancy's craving one of Hannah's baked goodies.
Can you help her find something to eat?**

*Find the twelve yummy baked goods in the letters below. They can be
forward, backward, up, down, or diagonal.*

BLONDIE

BLUEBERRY BUCKLE

BROWNIE

CREAM PUFF

CRISP

COBBLER

CUPCAKE

DOUGHNUT

ÉCLAIR

LEMON BAR

POPCORN BALLS

PFEFFERNUSSE

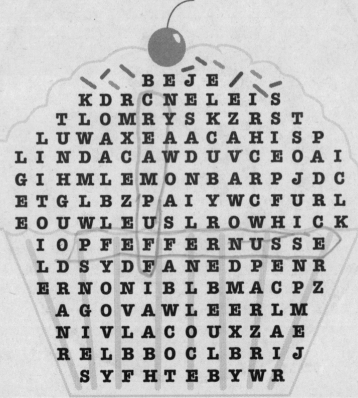

```
          B E J E
      K D R C N E L E I S
    T L O M R Y S K Z R S T
  L U W A X E A A C A H I S P
  L I N D A C A W D U V C E O A I
  G I H M L E M O N B A R P J D C
  E T G L B Z P A I Y W C F U R L
  E O U W L E U S L R O W H I C K
    I O P F E F F E R N U S S E
    L D S Y D F A N E D P E N R
    E R N O N I B L B M A C P Z
    A G O V A W L E E R L M
    N I V L A C O U X Z A E
    R E L B B O C L B R I J
      S Y F H T E B Y W R
```

LIES AND DECEIT

Two or more players

Play this game with a partner or group, anytime, anywhere. It makes waiting in line at the movies tons more fun! Be prepared for odd looks from bystanders until you ask them to play.

One person starts by pointing to a body part and saying, "This is my _____." Fill in the blank with the name of a different body part. For instance, you might point to your nose and say, "This is my knee." Player #2 must respond by pointing to his knee and calling it something else. Continue back and forth or around the group until someone makes a mistake (it won't be long!). Players are eliminated until a winner is apparent, or a score can be kept between two players.

Example:

Point to nose. "This is my knee."

Point to knee. "This is my eye."

Point to eye. "This is my elbow."

TO THE RESCUE (ASAP)

Nancy Drew knows how to do it. Do you? You want to know this so well you can do it in a heartbeat.

What do you mean you don't know what it is? Color every block below that has three sides— and only three sides— to find out.

Ask your friends to provide words to fill the holes in this story.

The thug was standing on the _____! I had him!
                              noun

The police were _____ around, shouting
                verb ending in "ing"

"_____," but that thug wasn't going anywhere.
  exclamation

Finally, I got my hands free from the _____,
                                       noun

so I could get the thug's _____ out of his
                          weapon

_____. That was _____,
article of clothing   *adjective*

let me tell you. Have you ever _____ one? It's
                               verb, past tense

_____. Anyway, the thug was _____, and he
   adverb   *emotion*

threatened to _____ me, but I didn't see how that
              verb

would happen since his _____ were all over the
                       plural noun

_____. Eventually, I got hold of the Chief on the
pieces of furniture

_____ and told him where to find us. That thug will
plural noun

be _____ _____ for _____ at _____.
   verb ending in "ing" *plural noun*   *number*   *US destination*

13

ND SPELLING BEE

Use Nancy Drew's initials—ND—to make words in the cells below, by adding them to the two letters in each cell. Find your way through the maze by connecting the real words (XRND is not a real word!) from beginning to end.

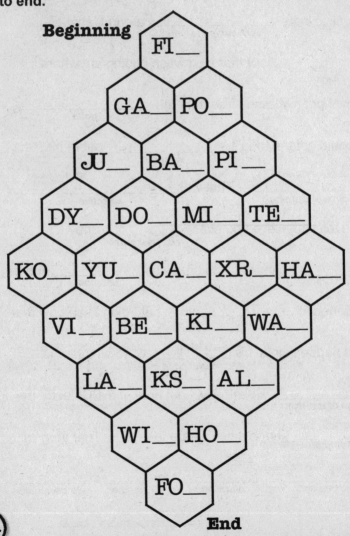

Beginning

FI__

GA__ PO__

JU__ BA__ PI__

DY__ DO__ MI__ TE__

KO__ YU__ CA__ XR__ HA__

VI__ BE__ KI__ WA__

LA__ KS__ AL__

WI__ HO__

FO__

End

14

DRAGON PENCIL PAL

Nancy makes a dragon bow to reveal a secret compartment. Put a dragon on your pencil, make it bow, and reveal some secrets of your own!

Materials

- Sculpey Eraser Clay (any color)
- Pencil (must be real wood)
- Toothpick

BODY

1. Form 3 balls of clay with these diameters: 1 inch, $1/2$ inch, and $3/8$ inch.

2. Roll the 1-inch ball into a 5 $1/2$ inch "snake," making one end (head) bigger and tapering down for a tail.

3. Pinch a ridge of points on the top side of the snake, beginning about $1/4$ inch back from head.

4. Pick up the snake. Keeping the ridge up, press the body lightly to the top of a pencil eraser about 1½ inches from head end of the snake. Bend the "neck" up, and tip the "head" down.

5. Create a loop in the body of the dragon, away from the pencil, then press the beginning of the "tail" to the pencil below the eraser.

6. Wrap the remainder of the tail around the pencil.

continued on next page…

FRONT LEGS

7. Split the 3/8-inch ball of clay into two halves. Roll each half into a thin cone shape, about 1 inch long.

8. Attach the thick part of each leg to the dragon where it sits on the pencil's eraser, so the points of the cones point up.

9. Bend the legs down, and press the ends, to form feet, against the pencil.

BACK LEGS

10. Repeat step 7 with the 1/2-inch ball of clay.

11. Attach back legs where the dragon's body comes back to the pencil after the loop. Use the technique in steps 8 and 9.

FACE

12. Poke 2 small holes for eyes with a toothpick.

BAKE

13. Bake according to package instructions. Cool and use!

Use your detective skills to uncover this movie dialogue, then guess who says it.

The letters in each column fit in the boxes directly below them. You decide which letter goes in which box. Each letter is used once. Black squares separate words, and the words wrap from one line to the next. Some of the letters are filled in to get you started.

I ~~O~~ L Y	N T	E G M	E ~~O~~ ~~R~~	~~A~~ ~~E~~ T ~~R~~ T	A I I T	I L T	E ~~L~~ S W	H S Y	E S	G ~~N~~ O T	E O	R S ~~T~~	K ~~O~~ S U	D I M	E E ~~L~~ M
		■	R			L	■				T	■			
	■		A	■				N				O			
O		■		R			■		■						L
	■		■		■			■		■					

Whose line is this? _____

17

SOMETHING IN COMMON

The six characters below have something in common.

Place each name on a line in the grid using the letters provided (and a little logic) to determine where each goes. There can be spaces before and after names, but not between letters. If you place the names correctly, what these characters have in common will be revealed in the highlighted column.

									E
		N							
				N					
		A							
L									
					Y				

ALLIE   LESHING

BIEDERMEYER LOUIE

JANE   NANCY

ANSWER: _____

Ned wants to meet Nancy alone, but Corky keeps showing up. So Ned makes a secret map that he hopes only Nancy will be able to figure out.

To follow this map, Nancy must obey the arrow signs. If an arrow points in one direction, she must continue in that direction until she comes to another sign. If there are two arrows in one box, she may choose to go either direction. Nancy's already figured out that she's supposed to start at the "†T." That Ned's a clever guy—no wonder she likes him! Where does Ned hope to meet Nancy?

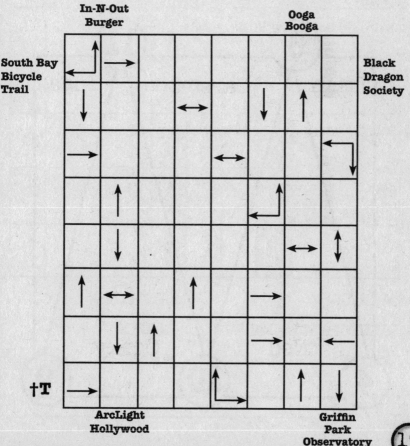

The lemon bars Hannah sent to Hollywood have disappeared. Nancy didn't eat any, but Carson, Ned, Corky, Trish, and Inga did. Each person ate from one to five bars, but no two people ate the same number. Numbers in the circles are the total bars eaten by the people whose sections meet at that circle. For example, Corky and Inga ate nine of the bars between them, while Trish, Ned, and Carson ate a total of six.

How many bars did each person consume?

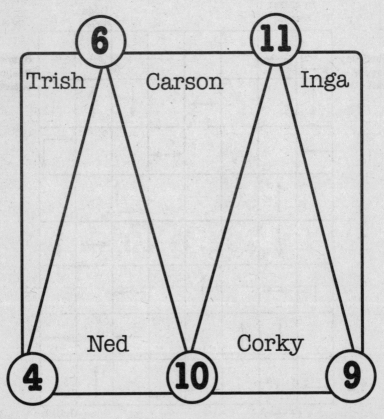

Use the Morse Code key to decipher a quote from the Nancy Drew movie.

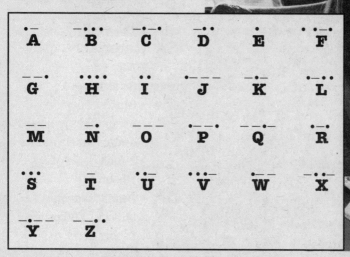

A ·—	B —···	C —·—·	D —··	E ·	F ··—·
G ——·	H ····	I ··	J ·———	K —·—	L ·—··
M ——	N —·	O ———	P ·——·	Q ——·—	R ·—·
S ···	T —	U ··—	V ···—	W ·——	X —··—
Y —·——	Z ——··				

·— —· / ·— — ·—· ——— ·—·· ——— ——· —·—— /

—— —— —— —— —— —— —— —— —— —— ——

·· ··· / — ···· · / ··· ·· ——· —· / ——— ·—· /

—— —— —— —— —— —— —— —— —— —— —— —— —— —— ——

·— / ——· · —· — ·—·· · —— ·— —·

—— —— —— —— —— —— —— —— —— —— ——

Who said it? _____

21

Tie this clever tag to your sleuth kit, and keep your ND Code Key safely on hand.

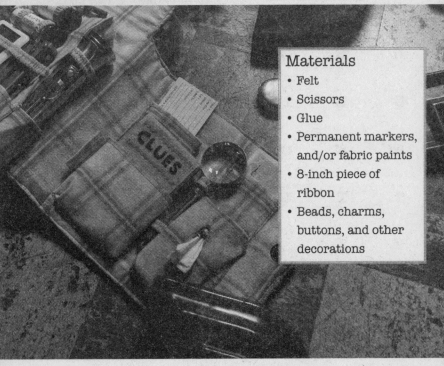

Materials
- Felt
- Scissors
- Glue
- Permanent markers, and/or fabric paints
- 8-inch piece of ribbon
- Beads, charms, buttons, and other decorations

1. Trace or cut out patterns on opposite page.

2. Cut one of each from felt.

3. CAREFUL! Poke hole in large felt piece where shown using scissors, a needle, or other sharp pointed object.

4. Glue 3 edges of smaller rectangle to larger tag. DO NOT glue the short side closest to the tag's hole.

5. Thread ribbon through hole and tie.

6. Decorate your tag with markers, paints, beads, charms, buttons, etc.

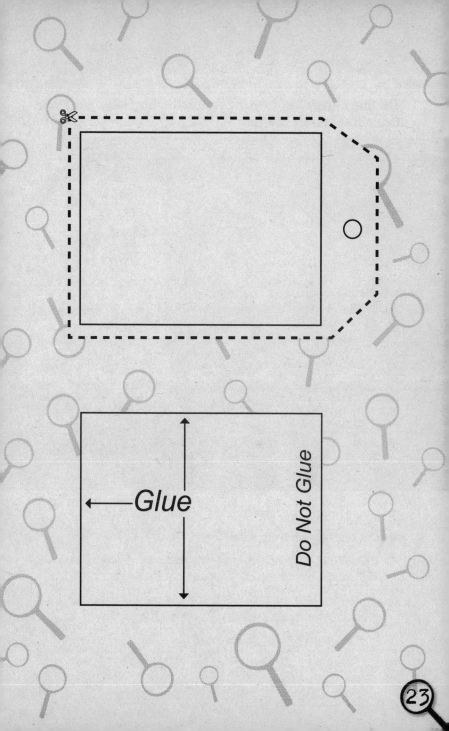

Glue

Do Not Glue

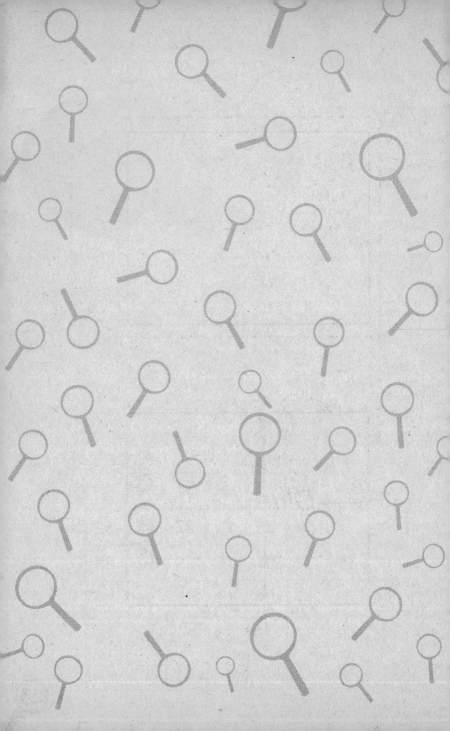

HOUSE HUNT

Nancy's on her way to meet a witness in her latest case. Unfortunately, she wrote the house number in her Pee-Chee folder, which was stolen. She remembers a few things about the number, but not the number itself. Can you help her find it?

The house number . . .
- Appears only once on the grid.
- Has an odd digit and an even digit.
- Does not end in 0.
- Has a second digit larger than the first.

64	77	90	43	76	91	57	31
50	16	65	24	82	67	42	87
84	99	80	61	16	11	94	66
29	17	39	53	10	27	48	52
91	40	32	51	75	35	97	68
86	70	42	87	93	62	36	72
18	59	67	27	60	39	53	18
26	13	41	22	97	73	29	30

Nancy is on the trail of four thieves. One of them has stolen a priceless diamond. When they give their statements, *only one of them tells the truth; the other three lie.* Nancy knows who is telling the truth, and who has stolen the diamond. Do you?

(Hint: If Harry's statement is true, are all others false? Remember, only <u>one</u> statement can be true!)

Harry: "Furley stole the diamond."

Joe: "Harry stole the diamond."

Furley: "Harry lied when he said I stole the diamond."

Champ: "I didn't steal no stinkin' diamond."

Pretend Inga is Simon and do what Inga says—and only what Inga says. If you're successful, you'll discover . . . well . . . something that Inga says!

	A	B	C	D	E	F
1	BTW	She's	Peek	This	The	Totally
2	Cupcake	It's	Is	BRB	Realize	As
3	I'm	We	Week	Insane	It's	Extreme
4	Label	Nice	Geek	LOL	As	Spastic
5	OMG	We've	I	MYOB	Awesome	TSTB
6	Get	Chic	Creek	XLNT	Freak	Righteous

1. Inga says, "Cross off every contraction in row 3 and column B."
2. Inga says, "Cross off all the words in row 6 and column C that rhyme with 'sneak.'"
3. Cross off every word with three letters or less.
4. Inga says, "Cross off every word ending with 'e' in row 3 and column E."
5. Inga says, "Cross off all the words with more than four letters in columns A and F."
6. Inga says, "Cross off every text message abbreviation in column D and row 5."
7. Inga says, "Read the remaining letters to read the best line in the whole movie."

Answer: _____ _____ _____ _____

_____ _____ _____ _____.

Nancy first demonstrates her emergency medical training by performing the Heimlich maneuver on Corky. What is Corky choking on?

To find out, read the letters above the numbers in order from 1-7. As it appears below, R, N, R, I are the letters above 1, 2, 3, 4. Since this is not the beginning of any word, mentally slide the number string to the right until you find the choking hazard by reading the letters in order from 1-7.

N	I	O	R	B	R	T	E	P	L	E	Z	L	W

2	4	6	1	7	3	5

Answer:

____ ____ ____ ____ ____ ____ ____

Nancy Drew can spot a fake. Can you?

Five of these pictures are of the same block in different positions. One picture is of an entirely different block. Which is the different block? (Hint: The polka dots are on the opposite side of the block from the diamonds.)

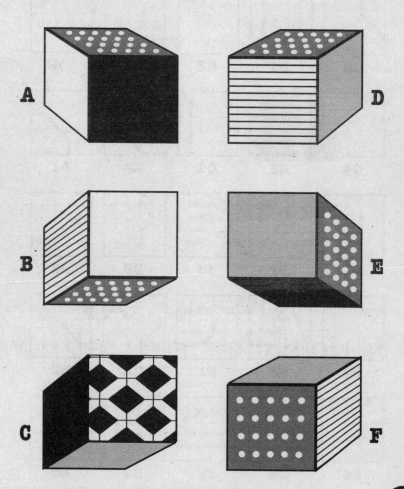

Copy the puzzle pieces below into the correct square on the grid to create a picture. The correct square is the one where the letter and number below each piece intersect.

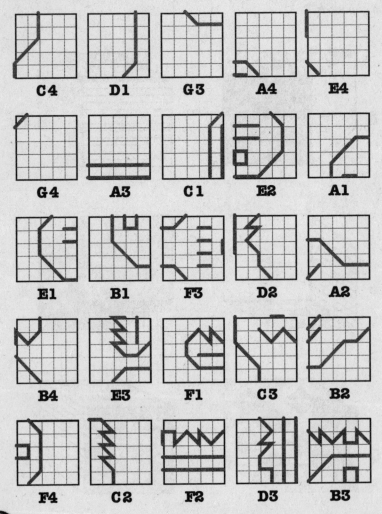

C4   D1   G3   A4   E4

G4   A3   C1   E2   A1

E1   B1   F3   D2   A2

B4   E3   F1   C3   B2

F4   C2   F2   D3   B3

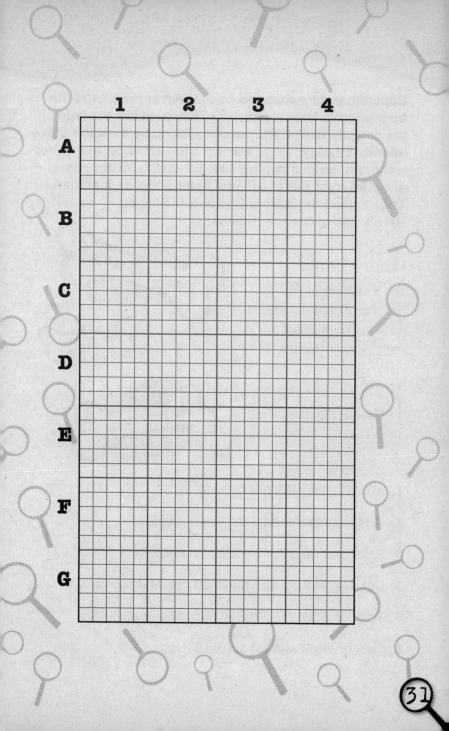

Remember the two thugs back in River Heights at the beginning of Nancy's movie? They held her hostage in the church. Well, Nancy made a mental note when Steve admitted that he never wanted a life of crime, but rather wanted to open a dog bakery. So when she got home, and Steve got out of jail, she helped him do just that! They named the bakery Chock-ful-O-Mutts! Here's one of Steve's recipes:

Ingredients
- ¾ cup beef broth
- ¼ cup cooking oil
- ½ cup powdered milk
- 1 packet yeast
- 1 egg
- 3 cups flour
- Cookie cutters

1. Mix dry ingredients in bowl.

2. Add liquids and stir until well blended.

3. Press out on counter to ½ inch thick.

4. Cut out cookies and place on greased cookie sheet.

5. Bake at 325°F for 35-45 minutes, until brown.

6. Cool on rack and let sit until hard.

Mirror, mirror on the wall, what's so funny, after all?

Black out the letters on the top half of the grid that have incorrect mirror images in the bottom half. Remaining letters reveal a funny movie quote. Do you know who said it?

```
WASCHEOKEBESPSF
TINLMDINNEGFRWE
SKHAXCNDEXDECIT
MIPNGWWAIUYSTOV
WEBTEAFKMRENAAK
```

Whose line is this? _____

Nancy needs you to search each square below. You're looking for a hidden will—and you need to do it fast.

*To get the job done quickly, draw a line from **Start** to **Stop**, passing through every open square **just once**. You can move up, down, left, or right, but not diagonally. Now get hunting, will you?*

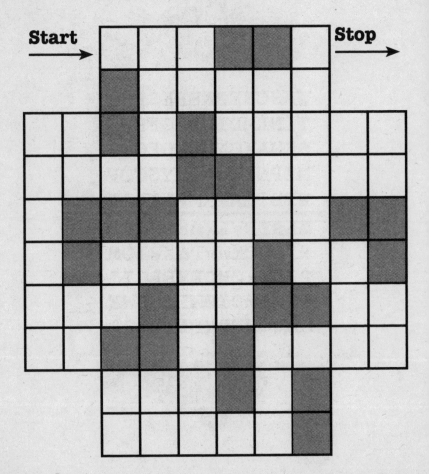

Start →

Stop →

Nancy would like the principal of her new high school to address some important issues. One is written below. What is it?

(Hint: It helps to hold the page at eye level.)

Answer: _____

Nancy Drew is determined to find out what happened to Dehlia Draycott.

Follow the clues carefully to uncover a mysterious connection.

1. Print the name
   DEHLIA DRAYCOTT.

1. _____

2. Delete the consonant that
   comes earliest in the alphabet.

2. _____

3. Switch the fourth and fifth
   letters from the left.

3. _____

4. Change the R to an N.

4. _____

5. Delete the first and last
   consonants from the right.

5. _____

6. Change the T to a J and the
   H to an L.

6. _____

7. Replace the ninth and tenth
   letters from the left with the
   same letters that are
   seventh and eighth from the left.

7. _____

8. Add an E after the third letter
   from the right.

8. _____

9. Switch the second and third
   letters from the left.

9. _____

10. Write all the letters in
    reverse order to make
    a connection to Dehlia Draycott.

10. _____

Ask your friends to provide words to fill the holes in this story.

The nerve! _____ stole my _____ right out
person's name .... _food_

from under my_____ ! I know s/he did it because I
.... _body part_

saw_____on his/her clothing. You know what
plural noun

I'm going to do? I'm going to _____
.... _food prep technique_

a special _____ tomorrow. I'll leave it in the
.... _repeat food_

_____ because s/he's always _____
place within a school .... _verb ending in "ing"_

around in there, so s/he's sure to _____ it. Then,
.... _verb_

after s/he _____ it, s/he'll _____ all
.... _verb_ .... _funny made up word_

over, right in the middle of _____ ! Everyone will
.... _school class_

see what a _____ s/he is, once and for all. And
.... _animal_

that will _____ him/her to steal my _____.
.... _verb_ .... _noun_

STOP! THIEF!

**Four thieves committed four crimes in one week.
Help Nancy figure out who stole what when.**

*Use the chart to record facts as you discover them. Put an X in a
box if you can rule it out. Use an O if it's a match.*

	His mother's pocketbook	A kiss	A way	A stole	Tuesday	Wednesday	Friday	Saturday
HARRY								
JOE								
FURLEY								
CHAMP								

1. The kiss was the first thing stolen, and the pocketbook disappeared on Friday.

2. Furley committed his crime before Harry, but he didn't steal the stole.

3. Champ committed his crime on Wednesday.

4. Either Harry or Champ stole his mother's pocketbook.

5. Joe committed his crime on Friday, or stole a way.

Use the code key to decipher a quote from the Nancy Drew movie. The letters for NANCY are provided, can you figure out the rest?

A B C	D E F	G H I
⌐ , &	+ .⌐ #	L .L &L

J K L	M N O	P Q R
@ . &L	□ □ &□	: = &L

S T U	V W X	Y Z
⌐ . &L	; .L "	⌐ %

EXAMPLE:

N A N C Y

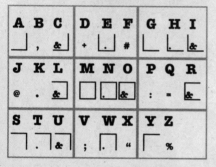

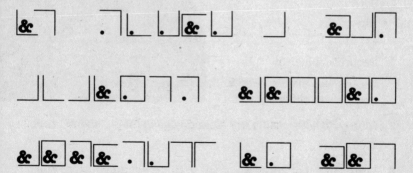

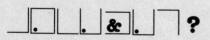

Nancy stays organized by keeping notes and clippings from each case in a Pee-Chee folder.

(That's a heavy-paper pocket folder. Pee-Chee was the name given to such folders when first released in 1943 by the Western Tablet and Stationery Company.)

Materials

- 1 Pee-Chee folder
- Clippings from magazines, cards, newspapers, or the computer
- Stickers, scrapbooking supplies, charms
- Movie ticket stubs (from Nancy's movie, of course!)
- Pens
- 1 large (1-inch) button for closure
- 11-inches of thin ribbon or cord
- Glue

1. Decorate folder by gluing clippings of images to describe folder contents.

2. Glue button to middle right-hand edge of folder, about 1 inch from edge.

3. Wrap ribbon or cord two or three times around button. Flip folder over. Pull ribbon taut to back, and glue in place. Allow to dry thoroughly before using.

A BUNCH OF BAD GUYS

Help Nancy Drew round up the bad guys!

A dozen desperados are hiding in the letters below. Find them forward, backward, up, down, and diagonally. Watch out, they're slippery! Every C, O, and N has been replaced by a ?. Can you nab all twelve thugs?

CONVICT	CRIMINAL	CROOK
DELINQUENT	FENCE	LOOTER
HOOD	MALEFACTOR	OFFENDER
OPERATOR	SHYLOCK	TRANSGRESSOR

```
? ? R ? ? K I L ? H S L
? H P E R ? T A R E P ?
? M Y E U M F E A L M ?
V F A L ? A D W R A X T
I D E L I ? Q U E ? T E
? K J P E E E L P I G R
T A ? F V F B F ? M R G
D W F ? I I A Z R I E ?
L ? S E L A M ? A R S V
V I ? T ? Y Q U T ? S I
? M A H V U H K H ? I ?
R ? S S E R G S ? A R T
```

41

Thanks to Nancy, Trish and Inga are dialed in to a new fashion trend. Crack this code to find out what it's called. Each number stands for one of the letters found with it on the telephone. You determine which one. A number may represent a different letter each time it's used. For instance, in N-A-N-C-Y (6 2 6 2 9), 2 represents A the first time it's used and C the next.

Trish and Inga's fashion trend:

8 4 3 6 3 9
7 4 6 2 3 7 4 8 9

___ ___ ___   ___ ___

___ ___ ___ ___ ___ ___ ___ ___ ___

What's the difference between a jeweler and a jailer?

To find out, start with a letter in one of the corners (no, we're not telling you which one), then read every third letter clockwise around the rectangle, until all the letters are used.

```
L T H L C E S H R O
T                 E
A                 W
E                 N
O                 S
W                 A
C                 E
E                 A
S                 T
S                 S
H L E T L H D E C N
```

Answer: ___ ___ ___   ___ ___ ___ ___ ___

___ ___ ___ ___ ___ ___   ___ ___ ___   ___ ___ ___

___ ___ ___ ___   ___ ___ ___ ___ ___ ___

___ ___ ___ ___ ___ ___.

Someone has stolen something off Nancy's bed!

To find out what was stolen, determine which letter of the alphabet is missing from each grid. Write the missing letter on the space below the grid. Then transfer the letters to the spaces at the bottom with the same numbers.

| G T N R U |
| K X I F A |
| Y D S C M |
| E Z V H Q |
| P L B W J |

| H T N Y L |
| R B W G Q |
| E O I M D |
| X K Z S V |
| F P U C J |

| L I P Z E |
| C R U H V |
| W F B N X |
| G Q J D S |
| O A K T Y |

| H Y O A W |
| S E U L Q |
| K V C X G |
| B P J R N |
| M F Z D T |

1._____   2._____   3._____   4._____

| E S L P B |
| X D Z J V |
| K R A W H |
| O F U M Y |
| I T C Q G |

| M W J U D |
| L G V E P |
| A O R Y I |
| S Z F N B |
| H X K T Q |

| N B U D K |
| I V H Q W |
| T F L A Y |
| C J M P G |
| R O Z E X |

5._____   6._____   7._____

Answer:

____ ____ ____ ____ ____ ____ ____ ____ ____
 3   1   6   6   2   7   4   5   7

Leave secret messages on your fridge, mirror, school locker, metal lunch box, or any place magnets stick.

Materials
- Magnet sheet or adhesive-backed roll, ½- or 1-inch width
- Scissors
- Markers or paint pens
- Paper (colored is nice)

Nancy—
Don't forget your sleuth kit!
-Ned

LESHING

WAS

HERE

1. If using magnet sheets with a surface that you can write on, write coded letters or words with markers or paint pens.

2. Cut out and arrange into words or sentences.

-OR-

1. If using magnets with an adhesive back, cut strips of paper slightly wider than the magnet.

2. Remove protective cover from magnet and press paper to sticky surface.

3. Trim paper even with magnet.

4. Write coded letters or words on paper with markers.

5. Cut apart and arrange into words and sentences.

Copy the key from the book and tuck it into the secret pocket in your Sleuth Kit Tag. Use the ND code to send and decipher secret messages.

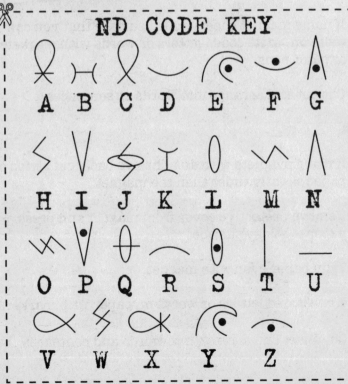

ND CODE KEY

A	B	C	D	E	F	G
H	I	J	K	L	M	N
O	P	Q	R	S	T	U
V	W	X	Y	Z		

Nancy received a gift. Want to know what it was?

Find the seven puzzle pieces that fit the spaces below. Pieces might be rotated or flipped. Write the letters of the correct pieces on the dashes. Not all of the pieces are used. When you've found the correct pieces, Nancy's special gift will be revealed.

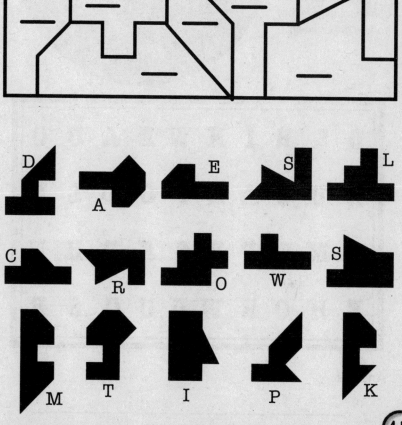

Corky was surpised by something Nancy ordered at the Chinese restaurant. What was it?

Cross off every letter that appears three times. Unscramble the remaining letters to find the answer.

D	S	R	I	H	W	E	A	C	O
N	U	C	A	N	P	O	U	L	D
A	M	W	P	E	S	K	P	H	N
E	H	O	R	W	D	U	C	S	R

Answer:

_____ _____ _____ _____

THE HOLE TRUTH

Sometimes there are gaps in a mystery and Nancy Drew has to fill in the holes. Fill in the holes below to find out what Nancy sometimes uses to piece clues together into a whole.

Add one letter to each word to make a new word that fits the clue. Write the letter you add in the box, then write those letters from top to bottom on the line below.

☐ TICK	Adhere
CO ☐ N	Nickel or dime
NE ☐ T	Following
☐ RAY	It holds plates and glasses
C ☐ OP	Cut into pieces
☐ HUT	Close
F ☐ AR	Alarm
LO ☐ G	Great distance
LI ☐ P	Speech problem
WE ☐ D	Dandelion or thistle

Answer: _____

49

It's that thug—the one with different-colored eyes, pale blue and black! He's after Nancy and her friends! Everybody RUN! The kids scatter throughout the mansion.

Can you figure out where everyone is hidden? Follow the vertical lines downward until you reach a horizontal line. Travel along the horizontal line until you reach another vertical line, then take that vertical line downward again. **You must take the new path at every intersection,** *always traveling down, left, or right. If you follow the paths correctly, you'll discover where Nancy and her friends are hidden. Let's hope you find them before the thug does!*

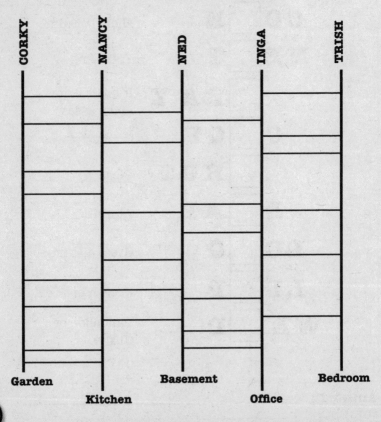

NEIGHBORHOOD SCAVENGER HUNT

Every item on this list is worth a certain number of points. Each person or team gathers as many items as s/he can in the allotted time. And just for the record, when we ask for a yellow car, we don't mean bring it back. We want to know where you found it, and maybe whose it is. Same with the bird's nest. 'Nuff said? When time is up, total the points, and crown a winner!

Item	Points
Acorn or nut	5
Animal footprint	20
Baseball glove	4
Berry	10
Bicycle helmet	10
Bird identification guide	10
Bird's nest	10
Bug spray	5
Candy wrapper	4
Clothespin	6
Coin found on the ground (no fair dropping your own!)	3
Crushed aluminum can	5
Empty milk container	2
Empty toilet paper roll	5
Feather	10
Fishing lure	10
Four leaf clover	30
Frisbee	5
Frog	20
Garden tool	5
Heart-shaped rock	10
Homemade chocolate chip cookie	10
House number with an 8	5
House with a red door	10
Hula hoop	5
Largest leaf	5
Leaf with insect holes	10
License plate with an X	10
Lipstick kiss imprint from a mother	30
Live insect	10
Longest blade of grass	10
Newspaper with the oldest date	10
Number of houses on your street	5
Number of windows in your house	5
Paper plate	5
Pencil tracing of the largest foot	10
Pencil tracing of the smallest hand	10
Piece of celery	5
Piece of charcoal	5
Piece of litter, not from a garbage can!	10
Pine cone	5
Pine needle	5
Plastic fork	5
Raincoat	10
Red hat	10
Red leaf	5
Safety pad (knee, elbow, etc.)	20
Seed from a tree	5
Sidewalk chalk	5
Sign (where is it, what does it say?)	10
Signature of canoe owner	10
Signature of someone with an April birthday	20
Signature of someone with white hair	10
Signature of the oldest person	20
Ski pole	10
Smallest leaf	5
Soccer ball	8
Something blue	5
Something orange	10
Something shaped like the number 4	10
Something that floats	5
Something that rolls	10
Something with a hole in it	10
Straw hat	5
Sunglasses	5
Tea bag	5
Tennis racket	5
Tent stake	10
Tire rubbing (lay paper on tire, rub pencil or crayon over it)	5
Tree rubbing	10
Turtle	20
Umbrella	5
Water from a swimming pool	7
Whistle	10
White rock	5
Worm	10
Yellow car	10

Total points: _____

Nancy wants to give you this message. She says it doesn't require instructions.

She says that you'll be right on top of the code and will follow the letters to make words back and forth, up and down, and all around. We're not so sure about that, but it's her book . . .

S	M	A	E	B	O	T	S	E	K
I	E	S	A	H	E	V	O	L	A
H	S	U	V	I	N	G	S	T	T
T	S	P	F	G	N	I	L	S	T
G	A	E	R	S	D	H	E	U	I
N	G	R	I	E	N	T	U	J	T
I	E	S	L	E	U	T	H	I	A
D	Y	O	U	H	A	V	E	W	H
A	E	R	E	R	'U	O	Y	F	I

START

52

NANCY DREW

ANSWERS

Page 3

I didn't realize it was a geek theme party.
                                                    —Inga

Page 4

Cathedral of Notre Dame

Page 5

Spies wear sneakers.

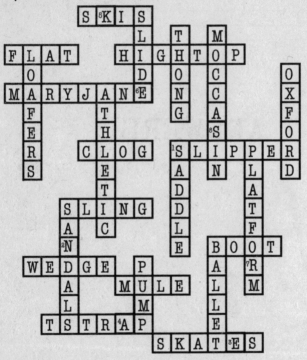

Page 6

PEE-CHEE FOLDER

Nancy

Leshing

FINISH

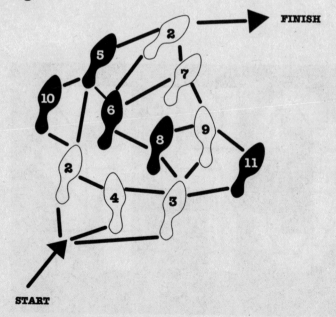

START

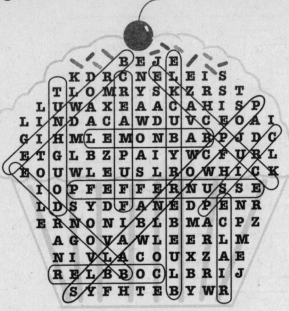

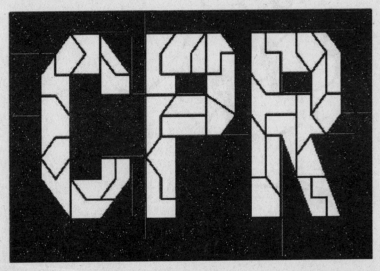

Page 14

BEGINNING

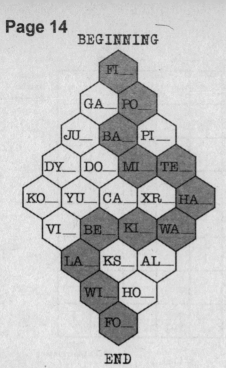

END

Page 17

It really gets my goat when someone tries to kill me. It's so rude.　　　—Nancy Drew

Page 18

B	I	E	**D**	E	R	**M**	E	Y	E	R
J	A	N	**E**							
L	E	S	**H**	I	N	G				
		A	**L**	L	I	E				
L	O	U	**I**	E						
		N	**A**	N	C	Y				

Dehlia Draycott is what these characters have in common.

Page 19

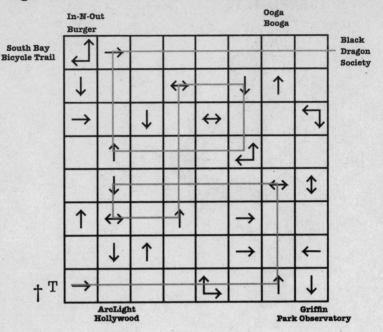

Page 20

Trish - 1

Carson - 2

Ned - 3

Inga - 4

Corky - 5

Page 21

An apology is the sign of a gentleman.

—Nancy to Corky

Page 25

36

Page 26

Only Furley's statement is true. Champ stole the diamond.

Page 27

BTW, this is as nice as I get.

—Inga

Page 28

PRETZEL

Page 29

Block A is the fake.

Page 30

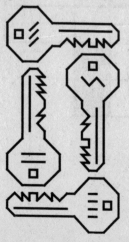

Page 33

She keeps finding fresh and exciting ways to be a freak.   —Inga to Trish

Page 34

Well, at least we know the will's not here.

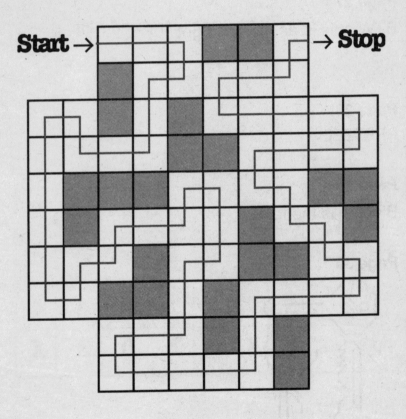

Page 35

Lead paint

1. Dehlia Draycott

2. Dehlia Drayott

3. Dehila Drayott

4. Dehila Dnayott

5. ehila dnayot

6. elila dnayoj

7. elila dnanaj

8. elila dnaenaj

9. eilla dnaenaj

10. **Jane and Allie**

Page 38

	His mother's pocketbook	A kiss	A way	A stole	Tuesday	Wednesday	Friday	Saturday
HARRY	O	X	X	X	X	X	O	X
JOE	X	X	O	X	X	X	X	O
FURLEY	X	O	X	X	O	X	X	X
CHAMP	X	X	X	O	X	O	X	X

Harry - Pocketbook - Friday
Joe - A way - Saturday
Furley - A kiss - Tuesday
Champ - Stole - Wednesday

Page 39

Is there a law against common courtesy in Los Angeles?　　— Nancy to Corky

Page 41

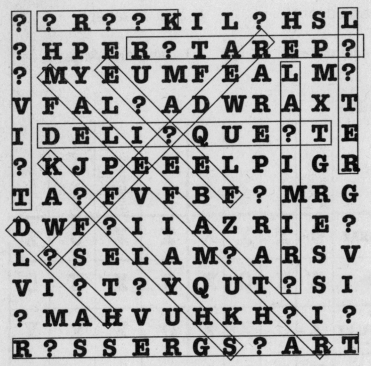

Page 42

The New Sincerity

Page 43

One sells watches and the other watches cells.

Page 44
Moccasins

Page 47
Ned gave Nancy a compass.

Page 48
Milk

Page 49
Sixth Sense

Page 50
Corky's in the garden; Nancy's in the kitchen;
Ned's in the bedroom; Inga's in the basement;
Trish's in the office.

Page 52
If you're reading this message you have what it
takes to be a super sleuth. I just love having
sleuthing friends!

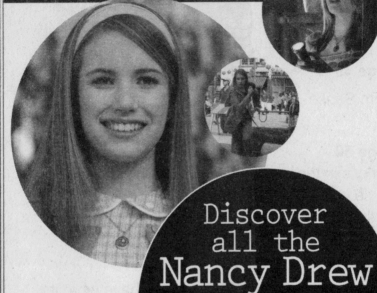